E
Tri Tripp, Valerie
Happy, happy Mother's
Day!

A JUST ONE MORE BOOK
Just For You

Happy, Happy Mother's Day!

by Valerie Tripp

Illustrated by Sandra Kalthoff Martin

Developed by The Hampton-Brown Company, Inc.

CHILDRENS PRESS®
CHICAGO

Word List

Give children books they can read by themselves, and they'll always ask for JUST ONE MORE. This book is written with 99 of the most basic words in our language, all repeated in an appealing rhythm and rhyme.

a
all
and
around
as
at

bag
begin
big
bloom
bought
but
by

came
could

day
did
Duck

enough

few
fine
flowers
for
four
Frog

garden(ing)
get
Giraffe
got
grew
grow(s)

had
happy
hardly
have
hello
her
home

I
in
into
it(s)

just

last
leaf
left
little

many
may
May

met
more
mother('s)
Mouse
my

neck
need

of
on
one
only
opened

plant(ed)
please
poor
power

reached
right

sad
say
seed(s)
she
some
spring

store
sunflower

take
that
the
then
there
three
till
to
too
took
two

very

walking
was
way
weed
went
what('s)
will
with
wonderful

you
your

1 2 3 4 5 6 7 8 9 10 R 94 93 92 91 90 89

Library of Congress Cataloging-in-Publication Data
Tripp, Valerie, 1951-
Happy, happy Mother's Day! / by Valerie Tripp ; illustrated by Sandra Kalthoff Martin.
p. cm. — (A Just one more book just for you)
Summary: Although generous Giraffe discovers with dismay that she has given away all but one of the seeds she bought to plant flowers for her mother for Mother's Day, she receives satisfaction in the end.
ISBN 0-516-01521-4
[1. Mother's Day — Fiction. 2. Giraffes — Fiction. 3. Animals — Fiction. 4. Stories in rhyme.] I. Martin, Sandra Kalthoff, ill. II. Title. III. Series.
PZ8.3.T698Hap 1989 89-35757
[E] — dc20 CIP
AC

Giraffe bought seeds one fine spring day
to grow a garden for Mother's Day.

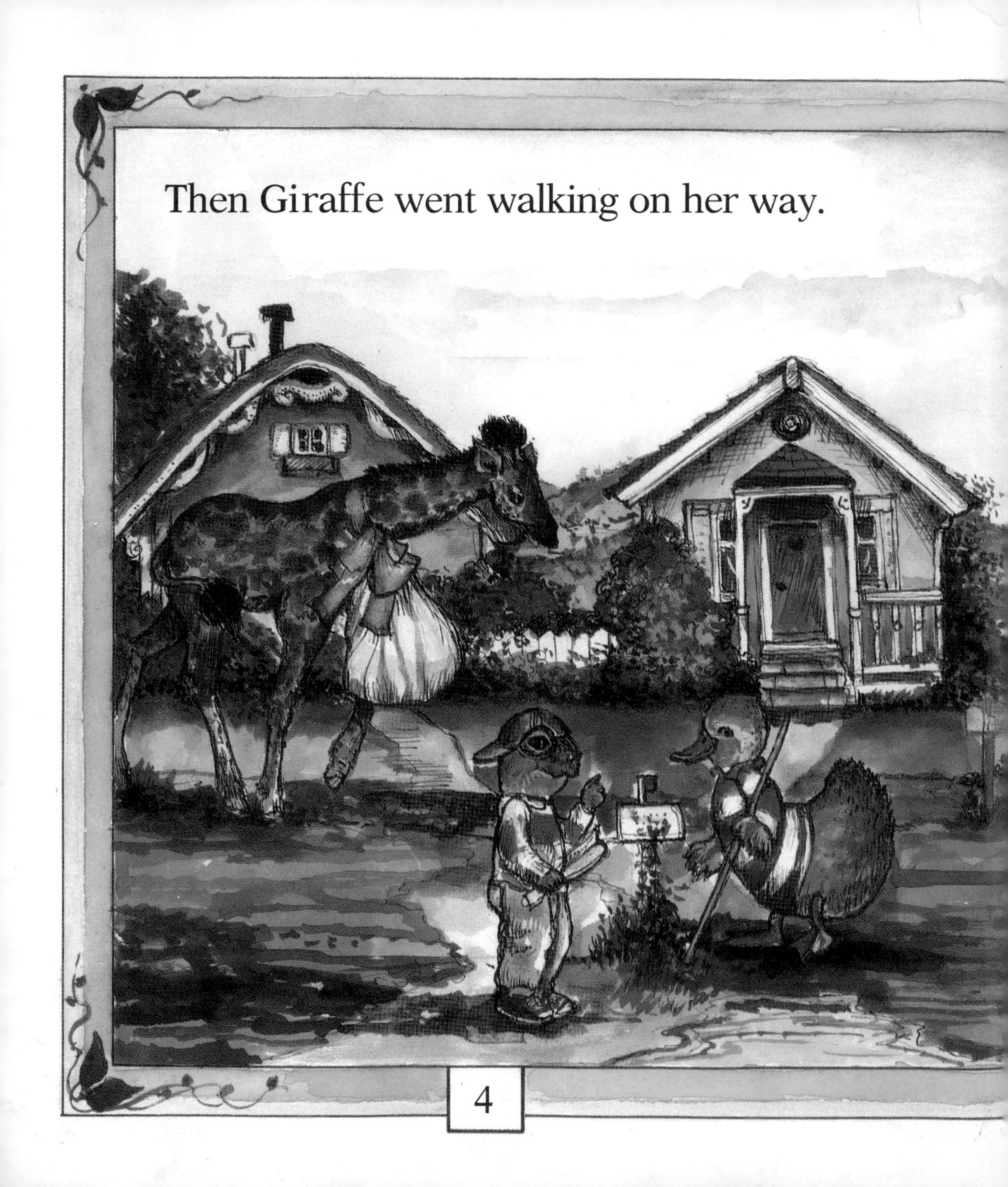

Then Giraffe went walking on her way.

And she met Frog
that fine spring day.

Hello, Giraffe!
What did you get?
What's in that bag
around your neck?

Seeds for flowers
to bloom in May,
all for my mother
on Mother's Day.

Please, Giraffe,
may I have a few?
I will grow flowers
for my mother, too.

Take as many
as you may need.

Frog reached right in
and took some seeds.

Then Giraffe went walking on her way,
and she met Duck that fine spring day.

Hello, Giraffe!
What did you get?
What's in that bag
around your neck?

Seeds for flowers
to bloom in May,
all for my mother
on Mother's Day.

Please, Giraffe,
may I have a few?
I will grow flowers
for my mother, too.

Take as many
as you may need.

Duck reached right in
and took some seeds.

Then Giraffe went walking on her way,
and she met Mouse that fine spring day.

Hello, Giraffe!
What did you get?
What's in that bag
around your neck?

Seeds for flowers
to bloom in May,
all for my mother
on Mother's Day.

Please, Giraffe,
may I have a few?
I will grow flowers
for my mother, too.

Take as many
as you may need.

Mouse reached right in
and took some seeds.

Then Giraffe went walking on her way,
till she came home that fine spring day.

At last her gardening
could begin.
She opened the bag
and reached right in.

But of all the seeds
she got at the store,
only one was left!
There was JUST ONE MORE!

Poor Giraffe was very sad,
but she planted that seed.
It was all she had.

Day by day,
what flowers grew

for Frog and Duck
and little Mouse, too!

Poor Giraffe had just one seed,
hardly enough to grow a weed.

But that little seed grew
one leaf, then two,

Then three, then four,
then just one more.

That little seed grew
with all its power.
It grew into . . .

a big SUNFLOWER!

What a wonderful way to say
Happy, happy Mother's Day!